NICKELODEON

Drake & Josh

NICKELODEON
Drake & Josh

Sibling Revelry

by Laurie McElroy
based on "Peruvian Puff Pepper"
written by Steve Holland and
"The Bet" written by George Doty IV

SCHOLASTIC INC.
New York   Toronto   London   Auckland   Sydney
Mexico City   New Delhi   Hong Kong   Buenos Aires

ISBN 0-439-83163-6

12 11 10 9 8 7 6 5 4 3 2   6 7 8 9 10/0

Printed in the U.S.A.

First printing, May 2006

Part One:
Sibling Revelry

Prologue

Drake Parker was stretched out on the couch in his living room with an open book on his lap. "Sometimes, when you plan to do one thing, something totally different happens," he said.

Josh Nichols hung out in his bedroom, practicing magic tricks. "Once I planned to ride my bike to the mall," he said, shaking his head. "I hit a bus."

"Oh, and there was the time I planned a surprise birthday party for Josh." Drake closed the book and sat up with a grin.

Josh fanned out a deck of cards facedown on the coffee table. "And I'll never forget the surprise party Drake planned for my birthday. . . ."

Drake made a note on his pad. "When he walked in, we all yelled, SURPRISE!"

Josh flipped the deck of cards over with one flick of his wrist. "I just wasn't expecting to be surprised by all those people in our room."

"Josh was so shocked, he threw a punch and nailed our Aunt Barbara right in the jaw." Drake laughed, picking up a set of drumsticks.

"I punched my Aunt Barbara." Josh grimaced. "But it was an accident." he explained.

"When she woke up, she was so mad, she took the present she'd bought for Josh and ran over it in our driveway." Drake stopped drumming on the coffee table and turned on the TV.

"And then she ran over my new cell phone." Josh said, stacking the cards. "With her truck."

"The whole thing was pretty hysterical," Drake said, changing channels.

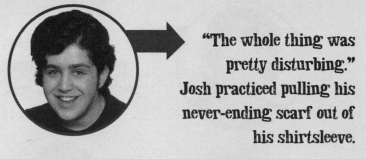

"The whole thing was pretty disturbing." Josh practiced pulling his never-ending scarf out of his shirtsleeve.

Drake played with a plastic Hawaiian doll someone left in the living room. "The point is . . ."

"The point is . . ." Josh got his hands tangled in the scarf.

Drake pushed the button on the bottom of the doll, and she did a hula dance. ". . . whenever you plan something . . ."

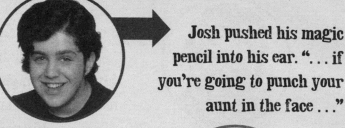

Josh pushed his magic pencil into his ear. "... if you're going to punch your aunt in the face ..."

"... don't be surprised when things take an unexpected twist." Drake made the doll dance again.

"... she just might run over your new cell phone." Josh pulled the pencil out of his mouth.

Drake sat back and laughed. "Yep."

Josh leaned back in his chair with a frown. "Yeah."

CHAPTER ONE

Josh Nichols checked the kitchen counter one more time to make sure he had all the ingredients for his recipe. With a huge smile, he smoothed his black-and-white striped apron and picked up one red, ripe, juicy tomato in each hand. He was ready.

"Time to make the salsa!" he announced. Josh crossed to the portable CD player on the counter in front of the pass-through window to the living room and pushed play.

"Welcome to *How to Make Salsa* with I, Horatio Hidalgo," said the voice on the CD. Horatio Hidalgo had a heavy Spanish accent.

Josh saluted the boom box and moved his hips in a happy salsa dance. "Hola, Horatio."

"First," said Horatio, "you must take time to appreciate your ingredients, as if they were a fine woman."

Tomatoes — a fine woman? But Josh had to follow the recipe. He checked out the tomatoes in his hands and, with an embarrassed expression, dropped them on the counter. "Sorry, ma'am," he said to the tomatoes.

Horatio Hidalgo continued with his instructions. "Now begin cutting your tomatoes into small chunks. I call this chunking the tomato."

"Chunking the tomato," Josh repeated enthusiastically. This was the fun part. He picked up a chef's knife and went to work.

Drake Parker, Josh's stepbrother, walked through the living room and saw Josh chunking his tomatoes. He also saw an excellent opportunity to pull a prank on his brother.

Drake and Josh were two guys with two different — totally different — personalities. Going to the same school used to be the only thing they had in common, but that changed in a huge way when Josh's dad married Drake and Megan's mom. Drake and Josh were suddenly brothers — and roommates.

Drake wasn't exactly thrilled about it at first. He was totally into having a good time — playing his guitar and hanging with his friends. He wasn't big on school — well, except for the girls — and he'd rather do anything than homework. He thought Josh was more than a little strange, especially in a geeky sort of way.

Josh was totally into following the rules — *all* the rules. Teachers thought he was the greatest. Not only did he do all his homework and study for tests — Josh did extra-credit assignments. In other words, Josh didn't exactly hang with the same high school in-crowd as Drake did.

But hanging with his cool, new stepbrother was one of Josh's favorite things to do. And Drake learned to like having Josh around — most of the time. One of the things he loved about Josh was how gullible the guy could be — like now.

Drake poked his head through the pass-through window and quietly pushed the stop button on the CD player. "But first," Drake said, imitating Horatio's deep voice and Spanish accent, "you must smell your tomato."

Josh looked confused. "Smell my tomato?" he asked.

"Inhale the aroma by pressing it to your nose with *great* force," Drake said, still imitating Horatio's accent. He emphasized the word "great" — urging Josh on.

Drake knew that his brother would follow the instructions exactly.

And Josh did. He shoved the tomato into his nose with great force, inhaling deeply. His eyes got wide. Juice splattered into his dark, wavy hair and dribbled down his face. Tomato seeds went up his nose.

Drake couldn't take it anymore. It was too funny. He cracked up, giving himself away.

Josh turned and saw him. *Oh great*, he thought. *Drake got me again.* "Cute," he said sarcastically, wiping his face with a towel. "Very, very cute."

"*Gracias, mi hermano*," Drake said in Horatio's voice as he walked through the door.

"Look, I don't have time for your jokes, all right? I have a lot of salsa to make," Josh said.

Drake was getting used to Josh's goofy projects, but salsa? "For what?" Drake asked.

"This year's big Salsa Fest." Josh did his spazzy little salsa dance again.

Salsa Fest? Is he kidding? But Josh didn't usually kid. "Whatever," Drake laughed.

"Hey, wait!" Josh said. He knew Drake wasn't exactly big on cooking — or any kind of work. But

Josh couldn't think of anything better than entering the contest with Drake. "I mean, if you want, you can be my salsa partner," he said hopefully.

"Wow! Wow! Really? I can?" Drake pretended to be super excited for about a second and then changed his tone with a shake of his head. "Well, that's not going to happen." He headed out of the kitchen, his shaggy, brown hair falling over his forehead.

Drake was wearing a yellow T-shirt with a funny diagram of the male brain. One huge section of the brain in the picture was devoted to rock and roll, Drake's first love. Another portion was devoted to television, which only left room for fast cars. In other words, he wasn't going to devote any brain power to salsa contests.

But Josh knew that Drake would stop mocking his salsa as soon as he learned what was at stake — the biggest, best plasma TV on the market. "Fine," Josh said. "But if you don't help me, then you won't win a forty-five-inch high-def Yatsabishi plasma screen TV," Josh said, stirring his salsa.

Drake slammed back into the kitchen. Had he heard right? "A Yatsabishi plasma screen TV?" he asked.

Josh nodded. "Mmm-hmm."

"Like a big one for our room?" Drake stretched his arms out wide.

"Mmmm-hmmm," Josh hummed again, bigger this time.

"Just for winning some stupid salsa contest?" Drake couldn't believe it. All he had to do to get a Yatsabishi for his room was chunk some tomatoes?

Josh danced up into Drake's face. His whole body answered. "Mmmmm-hmmmm!"

Drake would eat nothing but salsa for the rest of his life if it meant winning a free forty-five-inch plasma TV. He was on the salsa team! He pulled a cutting board toward him. "All right, would you stop humming? We have salsa to make!"

Josh grinned. How cool was this! The Parker-Nichols brothers were going to enter the Salsa Fest together — as a team. "Then start chunking the tomatoes!" Josh said.

"I'm chunking." Drake grabbed the big chef's knife and whacked a tomato. Unfortunately, it was way too close to Josh's hand.

Josh's jaw dropped in a silent scream.

Uh-oh, Drake thought. *That wasn't a tomato.* Drake grimaced and stopped chopping. "Should I get the first-aid kit?" he asked.

Josh stared at the knife. Then at his hand, his eyes wide. "Mmm-hmm."

CHAPTER TWO

Megan Parker, Drake and Josh's little sister, came into the kitchen and headed for the refrigerator. Josh chopped peppers on one end of the counter, a big bandage on his right pinkie. Drake chunked tomatoes a safe distance away. A big pot of salsa sat between them.

"Why are you guys making salsa?" Megan asked, grabbing a bottle of water.

Josh chunked a tomato. "So we can win this year's big Salsa Fest."

"And take home a high-def plasma screen TV," Drake said, now chopping some cilantro.

Megan's face lit up. "You mean one of those big flat screens that goes on the wall?"

Drake nodded. "That's right."

Wow! Megan would love to watch movies on a giant plasma screen TV. "Can I be on your salsa team?" she asked.

Drake and Josh exchanged "no way" looks,

then turned to Megan. "Nooooo," they said at the same time.

"Why can't I?" she whined. Her brothers never seemed to want her around. Why not? Was it just because she played a few tricks on them? What was a little hot sauce and itching powder between siblings?

"Well, because," Drake said. "When we win, that TV's going in our room." He knew that if Megan was on their team, she'd be in their room all the time watching that TV. Or worse — Mom and Dad would make them put it in the living room.

It was like Megan read his mind. "Why can't you put it in the living room so everyone can watch it?" she asked.

Josh shook his head. Couldn't she see that this was a brother thing? "Look, Megan, this is *our* thing." He pointed from himself to Drake and back again. "Why don't you go enter a cookie-baking contest or something?"

"Yes." Drake patted Megan on the head. "Run along now."

Megan narrowed her eyes. "Fine. I'll go." She turned

to leave the kitchen, but looked over her shoulder to have the last word. "Because I've got *things* to do," she said.

Josh was suspicious. The look in Megan's eyes made him nervous. He'd seen it before — like the time Josh was babysitting for his dad's boss, and the baby disappeared. Josh freaked. He tore the house apart and even climbed up onto the roof looking for the baby, but Megan had the baby safely hidden away all along.

"What things?" Josh asked.

Megan stopped and glared at them before pushing through the swing door. *"Things,"* she said.

Megan looked like a cute little girl dressed in pink with her big dark eyes and long, dark hair pinned back with flower clips. But she gave new meaning to the word "troublemaker."

She loved pulling pranks on Drake and Josh. Josh was definitely afraid of her — and for good reason. He knew that if Megan really wanted to be on their salsa team, she wouldn't give up that easily. She would plot her revenge.

Drake and Josh went back to chopping, but Josh was still worried. "What do you think she meant by 'things' to do?" he asked.

"Ah, man," Drake said. "She's just trying to scare us."

The only sound for the next few seconds was the thump of knives hitting the wooden cutting boards.

"What if she's in our room, doing something?" Josh asked.

Drake shrugged. "What could she be doing in our room?"

The sharp *thump, thump, thump* of the guys chopping went from fast to slow as they remembered all the things Megan had done in their room, from the time she let her pet snake loose to the time she sewed Josh's pajamas to his sheets while he was sleeping. Then they imagined the even more horrible things she could be doing right now. They dropped their knives.

"Megan!" Drake yelled.

"Get out of our room!" Josh added.

They stopped at the hall closet for weapons and shields and then raced upstairs.

As soon as the guys left the kitchen, Megan's head popped up from behind the pass-through window. Checking to make sure her brothers were out of sight, she darted into the kitchen and pulled a silver case out of her pocket. Megan dropped big yellow-and-red tablets in the salsa pot and giggled as she stirred. Her brothers were so easy to prank!

Drake and Josh rushed into their room. Josh leapt onto his bed and rolled off the other side with a tennis racket in his hand. He opened a closet door, ready to protect himself from whatever was about to jump out at him.

Nothing did.

Drake flipped couch cushions with a golf club, looking for anything deadly and dangerous.

Still nothing.

"Megan!" Drake yelled. He was convinced she was close by, ready to pounce. "What are you doing?"

Josh thought Drake needed him. He rushed to his brother's rescue, but he tripped on a sneaker and flipped over the couch. The tennis racket went flying, and Josh hit the floor. He jumped to his feet, ready to karate chop whatever threatened his brother. But Megan was nowhere in sight, and nothing had attacked them — yet.

The brothers stood back-to-back, surveying the room.

"Do you see her anywhere?" Drake whispered.

"No. But that's when she's the most dangerous," Josh answered, breathless.

They were ready to defend themselves and their room. But there was no Megan. No pranks. Their room was untouched.

Just then Walter Nichols, Josh's father, came into the room holding two ties. "Hey, guys, which of these ties do you —"

Startled by the noise, the guys screamed and whipped around to face Walter, tennis racket and golf club in hand.

Walter shrieked and ran out of the room.

Drake and Josh just looked at each other for a second, relieved and embarrassed.

"Great, we just gave Dad a heart attack," Josh said, panting.

"Yeah," Drake tossed his golf club on the couch. Dad would survive. They had a contest to win. "Well, back to the salsa," he said.

CHAPTER THREE

Megan stirred her brothers' salsa pot with a wicked grin on her pretty face. When she heard the guys coming, she put the spoon down and darted out of the kitchen, her long, dark brown hair flying behind her.

"I think we have some lemon juice in the fridge," Drake said.

"No, we have to use fresh lemons from the tree in the backya —" Josh cut himself off when he peeked into the salsa pot. It was bubbling. *Salsa doesn't bubble.* "What's up with the salsa?" he asked.

Drake stood next to Josh. The two of them stared into the pot.

"It's bubbling," Drake said.

Josh grabbed a wooden spoon and started to stir. What had Drake done? "You're not supposed to cook salsa, Drake," Josh said, eyeing his brother. "Did you turn the stove on?"

Drake looked at his brother like he was crazy. "Like I know how to work a stove," he said.

Josh checked the stove's dials, his forehead wrinkling in confusion. "That's weird. It's off," he said.

"Then why is it bubbling?" Drake asked.

Drake was a great guy, but he could be a little slow on the uptake sometimes. "If I *knew* why it was bubbling, would I be *wondering* why it's bubbling?" Josh said, sarcastically.

"Bubbling." Drake started to laugh as he said the word. "That's a funny word. Bubbling." He laughed again. "Bubbling."

Josh rolled his eyes. Drake was way too easily distracted from the mystery in front of them. You'd think the word "bubbling" was a pretty girl or something.

Megan sat between her mother and her stepfather in their cozy living room, watching television. And waiting.

Walter Nichols was the weatherman at KDLY, San Diego's most popular local news station. Josh was always cracking up at his dad's jokes. Megan thought her stepdad was a great guy, but when it came to his corny jokes, she wasn't exactly rolling on the floor laughing.

Audrey Parker-Nichols was a pretty cool mom who knew how to have a good time. She could hang with her kids as easily as she could hang with the grown-ups. But she had a serious side, too. Mostly, she really wanted everybody in her new family to get along.

Kaboom!

Their cozy family moment ended when the three of them heard a huge explosion in the kitchen. It sounded like a bomb!

Audrey grabbed her heart. Walter threw his body over Megan's to protect her. Megan simply grinned with a knowing look in her eyes.

"What was that?" Audrey asked.

Megan pretended to be surprised and scared. "I don't know," she said. With a big smirk on her face, she watched Walter and Audrey rush to the kitchen.

Audrey stopped short when she reached the door. "Oh . . . my . . . kitchen!" she screamed.

It looked like a salsa grenade had exploded. Drake and Josh were covered with tomatoes and peppers. The walls, cabinets, and even the ceiling were covered with dripping chunks of tomato and spices.

"What happened in here?" Walter asked.

"Well . . . umm," Drake sputtered.

"The, uhhh . . . salsa." Josh was too shocked to think of the word. He wiped salsa from his face.

"Exploded," Drake said.

"Yeah." Josh said, looking at the floor instead of his parents. He and Drake were in trouble — big trouble.

Walter threw his arms up in the air. "We can *see* that."

Audrey looked around, horrified. Just a few minutes ago, her kitchen had been clean. Now it looked like the aftermath of a super-scary horror movie. "Look at this place!" she yelled.

Drake tried to explain. "It wasn't our fault!"

"Oh, really?" Walter put his hands on his hips.

"Well, then, whose fault was it?" Audrey asked. She couldn't believe the guys were trying to get out of this one. It was their salsa — their explosion.

"I don't know," Drake said, pointing at the salsa pot.

"How are we supposed to know who . . ." Josh said at the same time.

The guys both realized at once. They looked at each other and then turned to their mom and dad. "Megan," they spat.

"Oh, so now you guys are going to try to blame this on your little sister?" Audrey asked. That was even worse than the mess the guys made.

"You two ought to be ashamed of yourselves," Walter added. "I mean, look how sweet she is, playing with her dolls."

They watched Megan through the pass-through window. She sat on the couch, pretending that her dolls were talking to one another. She looked up and gave a cute little smile and wave.

That would teach her brothers to leave her out of their salsa contest, Megan thought. But why stop there? It was time for Megan to do what she did so well — plan her revenge. She headed up to her room to get started.

Audrey fixed her eyes on Drake and Josh. "Now clean this up," she ordered.

Walter nodded in agreement and followed Audrey out of the kitchen.

Josh paced around the counter. He and Drake were both furious — they knew Megan was behind the exploding salsa, but they had no proof. And there was no way their parents would ever believe them without evidence.

"Man, I am so angry," Josh said, grabbing a towel to wipe his face. It would take hours to clean up this mess, and they were in trouble with Mom and Dad.

"You *know* Megan did this," Drake said.

"Yeah, I hate how Mom and Dad think she's soooo sweet," Josh said. "She's a demon, that's what she is." His voice rose with frustration. "A demon!"

"Yeah, she is," Drake agreed. He tried to run his hand through his hair, but it got stuck on a chunk of tomato. He was *so* tired of getting into trouble for things Megan did. "Hey, what if we give Mom and Dad proof about Megan?"

"What kind of proof?" Josh asked. Megan was too good. She always covered her tracks.

"I don't know." Drake thought for a minute. "But if we search her room, I bet we'll find some evidence."

The idea of searching Megan's room made Josh shudder. Who knew what kinds of weapons and booby traps she had hidden in there? It would be like stepping into enemy territory. "No. Uh-uh. She'll catch us, and then we'll get 'tazed' or something."

Drake was determined. "No. C'mon. We'll go look after school tomorrow when she's at oboe practice. She won't catch us."

Josh still looked skeptical, but there was no way Drake was going into Megan's room alone. He needed Josh's support, so he pushed a little harder. "Don't you want to prove to Mom and Dad that she's a demon?" Drake urged.

Josh looked at the salsa dripping from the walls. The salsa he would have to clean up. Megan had been getting away with too much for too long — not to mention putting pictures of his most embarrassing moments on the Internet. It was totally unfair. "Okay," he said. "Yeah! Let's do it."

They stared at each other like two soldiers about to go to war. They were still a team, only now they had a new mission: Operation Get Megan.

But all this talk made Drake hungry. And that salsa was looking good, even though it was splattered all over the kitchen. He grabbed a tortilla chip and used it to scrape some salsa off of Josh's face before eating it.

Josh stared at his brother, amazed.

Drake picked up another chip and started to do the same thing.

Josh slapped his hand away. "Will you stop it!" he yelled.

CHAPTER FOUR

Drake and Josh peeked around the corner and then tiptoed down the hall. They were dressed in black from head to toe, like ninjas.

"Let's do this," Drake whispered.

Josh stopped short, panicked. "Wait," he hissed.

"What?" Drake asked.

"I'm afraid," Josh said, cowering.

Drake gaped at him.

Afraid of what — a little girl's room? Besides, they had a plan. And now was the perfect time to put it into action.

"I've never been in Megan's room before," Josh said. "Have you?"

"Once, when she was five," Drake admitted.

Uh-oh. This didn't sound good. "And?" Josh prompted.

"She pushed me out the window, then told Mom I fell." Drake cringed, remembering.

"I'm out of here," Josh announced, heading down

the hall. Messing with Megan was dangerous. Messing with Megan in her own room had to be beyond dangerous.

Drake grabbed him by his sweatshirt and pulled him back. "Wait! She's at oboe practice. Now, c'mon!" Drake knew it was now or never. How often did he and Josh get the house to themselves? He opened Megan's door and poked his head in. The coast was clear.

Josh trembled in the doorway. He almost halfway expected to find himself caught in some kind of painful booby trap the minute he stepped over the threshold. Drake grabbed him and pulled him into the room.

It looked like a normal little girl's room — not a wicked witch's hideout. The walls were painted light purple. Decorative butterflies and flowers covered the walls. There was a fluffy pink rug on the floor, and pink and green pillows on the bed.

Josh held his hands up, karate style. So far there was nothing to protect himself from. But he didn't want to stick around one second longer than necessary. "Okay, now look around," he said. "Find some evidence that proves she's a demon, and then let's get out of here."

"Yeah," Drake shuddered. "This place gives me the skeeves."

They split up to examine the room. Drake looked in Megan's nightstand drawer while Josh peered under the bed.

"Do you see anything?" Josh asked. "Anything over there?"

Drake shook his head and headed for Megan's desk. He picked up a framed picture and stared at it for a few seconds. "Josh! Josh! C'mere!" Drake said.

Josh rushed over. Was it proof that Megan was as bad as Josh knew she was? "What?" he asked.

"Check out this family picture," Drake said.

Josh looked over Drake's shoulder, but didn't see anything unusual. Was there a clue hidden in the photo? "What about it?" he asked.

"I look gooood," Drake said, admiring himself with a grin.

Josh quickly snatched the picture frame and slammed it down on the dresser. "Will you please stay focused?"

Drake remembered why they were there — to gather evidence. "Okay!"

Josh continued his search. He couldn't find anything unusual — nothing to help prove that Megan was an evil demon. And she could come home from oboe practice any time. A thought crossed his mind that stopped Josh dead in his tracks: *What if she skipped oboe practice today and caught us in her room? Talk about dangerous.* They had to hurry. "See anything yet?" he asked.

Drake shook his head — nothing. But he knew there had to be something, somewhere.

Josh checked the wall behind Megan's pink bulletin board. "Check in the closet," he urged Drake. "Anything in there?"

Drake opened the closet door slowly and peeked inside. He pushed some clothes aside and jumped back, waiting for something to pop out at him. Nothing did. He poked around a little.

Josh ran his hands across a picture of unicorns and bunnies on the wall over Megan's dresser. He put his ear against the poster like a safecracker and ran his hand along the poster's top edge. He could hear a beeping sound. Something was behind this innocent-looking poster!

"Man, there's nothing in here," Drake said. "It just looks like a normal little girl's room."

"Oh, ya think?" Josh asked. He yanked the poster off the wall. There was a row of four closed-circuit TV monitors behind it, and a lot of flashing buttons and lights — even a radar screen. This was no normal little girl's room. This was something completely different.

"Whoa!" Drake yelled. It was a whole wall of high-tech spy gear. Where had Megan gotten all of this stuff?

"Holy cheese!" Josh said. "Look at all this equipment."

Drake crossed his arms. "So this is how she always knows what we're doing." He peered at all the buttons and lights. There was a big red button in the middle of the panel. "Hey, what do you think this button does?" he asked, pressing.

Bzzzztttt!

Josh jumped two feet in the air and grabbed the back of his pants. "So that's why that's been happening," he said, pointing at the red button. "I thought it was my electric personality."

Electric personality? Drake stared at him, speechless for a moment. Then he realized they were almost out of time. Megan would be home any second. "C'mon! Let's get this thing back up."

"Right," Josh said, hurrying.

They hung the poster back on the wall, covering Megan's spy gear.

"So what do we do now?" Josh asked.

"When Mom and Dad get home, we'll show them this stuff," Drake answered. "Then they'll see what Megan's really like."

They finished putting the poster back up.

"Yep. Because now we've got evidence, baby." Josh smiled and rubbed his hands together. Megan's days of being a spy master were almost over. Soon their mom and dad would know she wasn't the sweet little girl she pretended to be. "C'mon, let's get out of here."

The guys snuck out. But Drake wheeled around and picked up the family picture again with a pleased grin. He did look good.

Josh followed him. Drake could gaze at his picture any time. What if Megan came home and found them in her room? "Put. It. Down," he ordered. He waved his hand in the air, directing Drake out of the room and into the hall, before closing the door behind them.

CHAPTER FIVE

"Hello," Walter said.

"We're home," Audrey called.

Drake and Josh were stirring their salsa in the kitchen. They had changed out of their ninja clothes so Megan wouldn't be suspicious.

"They're home!" Drake put down his wooden spoon. This was it!

"Good! I can't wait to expose Megan for the evil little troll she is," Josh said. He rushed out of the kitchen, followed by Drake.

They ambushed Walter and Audrey in the living room.

"Mom! Dad!" they said. "Come with us."

"What?" Audrey said.

"What's going on?" Walter asked, confused. The guys seemed excited about something.

"You think Megan's a sweet little angel?" Drake said.

Josh grabbed his mom by the shoulders. "Prepare

to think differently!" he said. "Let's go." He grabbed Walter by the arm and pulled him upstairs. Drake followed, pushing his mom in front of him.

They burst into Megan's room seconds later, dragging a confused Walter and Audrey behind them. Megan sat on her bed, looking all innocent, knitting.

"Oh, hi," Megan said sweetly, holding up a yellow sweater and some yarn. "Look, Mommy, I knitted you a sweater."

Audrey put her hand on her heart and smiled at her sweet little girl. "Awwwww."

Drake had his arms crossed over his chest. "Oh, don't act all innocent, Megan."

"Yeah, your prankster ways are about to be exposed," Josh warned.

Megan looked at them, wide-eyed. "What do you mean?" she asked.

Josh pointed to the unicorn poster on the wall. "This is what I mean!"

"Do it, Josh," Drake said. He couldn't wait!

The guys kept their eyes on their mom and dad while Josh pulled the poster off the wall with a dramatic flourish and let it fall behind Megan's dresser.

And now Megan was exposed as the spying little trick-ster that she truly was.

Drake and Josh gestured over their shoulders toward the wall of spy equipment, waiting for their parents to take it all in. The guys gave each other high fives. Then they pointed toward the wall again.

But something wasn't right. In fact, something was very, very wrong. Mom and Dad were not reacting the way they were supposed to react. Walter and Audrey stared at them with blank expressions, and Megan had a smug little smile on her face.

Drake turned. His grin faded when all he saw was a blank purple wall. He grabbed Josh's shoulder and turned him around. The panel of high-tech spy equip-ment was gone!

Josh stared at Drake.

Drake stared at Josh.

Their parents stared at them.

Megan ran to Audrey and threw her arms around her waist. "Mommy, they knocked my poster down!"

Audrey petted Megan's hair. "It's okay, sweetie."

The guys signaled each other desperately with

their eyes. What happened? Megan had gotten the best of them — again! How did she do it?

Walter crossed his arms over his chest and glared at the guys. "Care to explain?" he asked.

Josh started to babble and point. "Okay, okay. There were monitors right there and . . . dials . . . oh and . . . and a little buzzer that hurt my bottom." His voice trailed off in embarrassment.

"It was all right there!" Drake insisted.

Drake and Josh ran their hands over the wall, desperately trying to find the monitors and buzzers.

"There was a radar thing," Drake said, desperately feeling for bumps in the wall.

"And buttons and lights!" Josh said.

Megan hugged Audrey and pretended to cry. "Why are Drake and Josh talking so crazy? I'm scared." She edged behind her mother.

Josh scratched his head, totally confused.

"Drake. Josh. In the living room. Now," Walter commanded.

They trudged out. Not only were they in trouble, but somehow Megan had managed to trick them —

again. Not only did they look bad. Megan made herself seem like a sweet little angel once more.

Megan watched her brothers leave, followed by Walter. She looked up at her mother with big, tear-filled brown eyes. "Why do people have to be bad?" she asked.

Audrey hugged her. "You just go back to your knitting, okay?"

Megan sniffled. "I'll try." She sat on her bed and pretended to reach for her knitting, but as soon as Audrey left the room, Megan's tears turned into a big smile. Did her brothers really believe she wasn't at least three steps ahead of them at all times?

She lifted a small picture from the wall and pressed a red button. The big purple wall slid silently away, revealing all of Megan's high-tech spy gear.

Megan ran to the wall and got her remote control. She pressed a button, and all four TV monitors on the wall came to life. With the touch of another button, all four monitors revealed pictures of Drake and Josh in the living room, getting yelled at by Dad. Megan leaned back on her bed and watched with a happy smile. That would teach them to search her room.

". . . calling you gentlemen like you're actual gentlemen," Walter ranted. "You're boys. The two of you. You're boys; you behave like children. Why would you do . . ."

Drake and Josh sat on the couch, their shoulders slumped and their heads down. Trying to defend themselves now was useless. Megan had pranked them again — big time.

Megan watched it all with a huge grin. "Poor little monkeys," she said.

CHAPTER SIX

Josh stumbled through the front door and into the living room, loaded down with four heavy grocery bags filled with tomatoes, peppers, and other salsa ingredients. Drake followed behind him, carrying a small plastic bag.

"Who knew tomatoes were so heavy!" Josh heaved the bags onto the table and wiped his forehead. "You know, you could've helped me," he said, turning to Drake.

Drake held up his baggie. "I got the cilantro."

Audrey came in from the backyard, carrying a garden trowel. "Hey, boys," she said.

"Hi, Mom," Josh answered, relieved she wasn't still mad at him about the exploding salsa.

"What's up?" Drake said.

Audrey picked up her gardening tools and gloves from the table. "Listen, I think it was really great of you guys to let Megan help you with your salsa."

Let Megan help them? Like that would ever happen. Drake and Josh looked at each other, then at their mom, confused.

"Huh?" Josh asked. Megan had already gotten back at them for saying no with the exploding salsa. What was she up to now?

"She's *not* helping us," Drake said. That TV was going right into his and Josh's room. No way was Megan getting in on the action.

"Yeah." Josh put his hands on his hips. "We told her no."

"Well, that's weird," Audrey said, as she headed out to the garden. "Because she's upstairs in her room with a whole bunch of salsa ingredients."

Josh's eyes got wide. Drake stopped in his tracks. *What was the little demon doing now?* They raced upstairs to find out.

Drake and Josh dashed into Megan's room. She had set up a makeshift kitchen on a table at the foot of her bed. Salsa ingredients and kitchen supplies were lined up, and a big pot of salsa was ready to sample.

"Whassup?" she asked, stirring her salsa.

"Okay, what are you doing?" Josh asked.

Megan smiled innocently and sprinkled some spices into her pot. They really were idiots if they thought she was going to give up that easily. That TV was hers. And if they didn't want to share, neither did she. "Making salsa," she said.

"Why?" Drake asked.

"Because I want to win the plasma screen TV," Megan said. "You guys wouldn't let me on your team, so I'm going to enter my own salsa." She didn't need to add the words "and win." That was a given. Megan held up a spoonful. "Want to taste?"

"Yeah, I do." Josh nodded and stepped forward. There was no way Megan's salsa was better than his.

Megan pulled the spoon back. "Too bad," she said sweetly, then she got tough. "Get out."

Drake pretended not to be bothered, but there was no way he would let Megan win that contest without a fight. "Okay, go ahead," he said. "Enter the contest. We don't care."

Megan picked up the salt. "Good."

"Good!" Josh added. He'd been cooking for years, and he'd never seen Megan make more than a peanut-butter-and-jelly sandwich. Let her enter. He would still win.

Josh turned to his salsa-making partner. "Let's get out of here."

He and Drake stormed out, but Josh stopped in the doorway with one last warning. "You know what? You just remember this one thing, little girl." Josh pointed at his chest. "I've been making salsa for five years."

Megan picked up a remote control and pressed a button.

Josh didn't notice. He was still talking. "So if you think you're going to beat Drake and me —"

Slam!

The door closed with a bang in Josh's face.

Megan shook her head and smiled. Josh was such an idiot.

After three marathon salsa-making sessions the next afternoon, Josh and Drake were ready to settle on the best recipe — the plasma TV–winning recipe. They sat on the couch in the living room with bowls of salsa and tortilla chips in front of them.

Josh tasted the last batch. "So what do you think?" he asked. He knew it was great salsa, but he wanted to hear it from someone else.

Drake crunched a salsa-covered chip. It tasted like a winner to him. "Awesome. This is the best salsa ever."

"We done good, brothah!" Josh said. "Knuckle touch."

Drake rolled his eyes. Josh always wanted to do the goofiest things, but it was easier to give in than fight. At least they didn't have to hug this time. He halfheartedly banged his knuckles against Josh's.

The doorbell rang.

"Who's that?" Josh asked. He stood up to answer the door.

"I don't know." Drake got up, too. They weren't expecting anyone.

Megan came bounding down the stairs. "Just sit down," she ordered. "I got it."

She opened the door to a man who looked like a

professor. He wore a suit and held a stainless steel briefcase close to his chest, like it was precious or something.

"Hi. Are you Miss Megan Parker?" he asked.

"Yeah," she answered. "Are you Pharnsworth?"

"Indeed." Mr. Pharnsworth held up his case. "So, I brought the Peruvian —"

Megan cut him off. "Shhhh." She looked over her shoulder at Drake and Josh, who stood near the couch, watching. "Let's talk in the kitchen," she said to Mr. Pharnsworth.

"Hey," Drake said, curious, "who is that guy?"

"None of your bees' guts," Megan answered.

Josh and Drake watched Megan follow the man into the kitchen. *What was she up to?* they wondered. *And did it have anything to do with the salsa contest?* Drake signaled Josh to squat down. They waddled over and hid under the pass-through window so they could hear every word.

"Okay, let's see what you've got," Megan said excitedly.

"Very well." Mr. Pharnsworth set his case on the kitchen table and opened it slowly. Then he pulled out a lunchbox and opened that, showing Megan what was inside — a bunch of colorful red and green peppers.

Megan gasped and put a hand over the purple paisley butterfly in the middle of her pink T-shirt. "Oh my goodness!" She took a pepper and held it up to the light to admire it. "The Peruvian puff pepper," she said, awed.

Drake and Josh peeked over the counter, then ducked down again.

"Yes, these are among the finest specimens in the world," Mr. Pharnsworth said. "The pinnacle of peppers, if you will." He chuckled to himself.

Pinnacle of peppers? Megan stared at him. *What a geek!* she thought.

He stopped chuckling. "I'm a botanist," he explained when he saw her expression.

Megan still thought he was a geek. "So how much for the peppers?" she asked.

"Fifty," Pharnsworth answered.

"Dollars!" Megan yelled. *Fifty dollars? For peppers?*

Pharnsworth nodded. "Young lady, these are the rarest peppers known to mankind. I'm afraid it's fifty dollars or no deal." He crossed his arms over his chest.

Megan was no fool. She knew how to negotiate. "Forty," she said firmly.

Mr. Pharnsworth nodded. "Forty," he agreed.

Megan handed over two twenty-dollar bills and then slid the peppers into a paper bag.

"Thank you." Mr. Pharnsworth slipped the cash into his briefcase. "So, what are you making?" he asked.

"Salsa — for a contest," Megan answered.

"Well, if you put these peppers in your salsa, you'll win for sure."

Drake and Josh eyed each other. Megan couldn't win! That was *their* forty-five-inch high-definition Yatsabishi plasma screen TV.

Megan had a devious look on her face. "I know," she said.

Mr. Pharnsworth gathered his stuff together. "Well, I better go. I've got a big date tonight."

Megan looked at him. Even Josh could get a date before this guy, she thought. "Dinner with your mom?" she asked, sarcastically.

Mr. Pharnsworth deflated like a burst birthday balloon. "Yes."

Megan smiled.

Pharnsworth headed for the front door while Megan headed upstairs with her peppers.

Drake and Josh stayed hidden. If Peruvian puff peppers were what it took to win the salsa contest, they'd have to find a way to get some.

CHAPTER SEVEN

Josh stood behind the counter at The Premiere. He wore his uniform — a red vest with a giant P on the lapel over a light blue shirt. The Premiere was a movie theater, and since Josh worked there, Drake knew he could talk Josh into letting him into movies for free once in a while.

"Thanks," Josh said to a woman as he handed her a big bag of popcorn. "Enjoy the movie." He put the cash into the register.

Drake was standing at the counter, using a laptop with wireless Internet access.

"So what does it say about the pepper?" Josh asked.

"Let's see." Drake tapped a few keys. "It says, 'The Peruvian puff pepper. Grown only in the north-western mountains of Peru, this extremely rare pepper is highly desirable for its exotic, sweet taste, and spicy heat.'"

"Okay, so how do we buy some?" Josh asked. There was no question about it — their salsa had to beat

Megan's, and they needed Peruvian puff peppers to do it.

Drake clicked a few more keys. "Can't," he said, checking the screen. "Says here, they're only available in South Ah-meer-eek-a."

Josh stared at Drake, openmouthed. Was he kidding? Or was he really that clueless?

Drake knew that look on Josh's face meant something. "What?" he asked.

Uh-oh. The answer was he *was* really that clueless. "South *America!*" Josh yelled.

Drake looked at the screen again. Then it dawned on him — he *had* seen that word before. "Oh," he said with a nod. "South America."

Josh slammed his hand down on the snack counter. The real problem wasn't pronunciation. It was the fact that Megan had a secret ingredient, and they didn't. "Stupid puff pepper," he said. "We can't let Megan win that plasma screen! What are we going to do?"

Drake closed the laptop. He had an idea — an *excellent* idea. "I'll tell you what we're going to do." He leaned in closer so no one would hear. "We're going to steal Megan's peppers."

"We can't do that!" Josh said.

"Give me one reason," Drake said.

Josh shrugged. They just couldn't. It wasn't right. "It's mean," Josh said, finally.

Mean? Was Josh *serious*? "Josh, think back," Drake urged. "Can you think of a couple of mean things Megan's done to us in the past few years?"

A couple? Josh had a long list. He thought back to all of the mean things Megan had done to him — jumping up behind him and scaring him, exploding guitars, shaving cream on his nose while he was sleeping, the corn dog that blew up in his face, mud-filled water balloons, tricking him into gluing himself to a chair. Not to mention the exploding salsa. And then there was the absolutely worst thing — the time she had psyched him out so bad that he turned into a giant, twitching mess on the TV news. It took a long time for Josh to get over that one, even with Drake's help.

"Well . . ." Drake said, encouragingly.

Josh's eyes narrowed with determination. "Let's steal her puff peppers."

* * *

During oboe practice the next day, they had their

opportunity. Drake and Josh, dressed in their black ninja spy shirts, pants, and hats, crept down the hall and into Megan's room. Josh opened the door and swaggered in like he owned the place. No cowering on the threshold for him this time — he had a mission. He would get those Peruvian puff peppers, and he and Drake would win that TV.

Then he remembered — this was Megan's room, the place where she dreamed up all of her evil tricks. He stopped short. She could be watching him right now.

"Okay, there's the bag!" Drake whispered from the doorway. He pointed to the paper bag they had seen Megan slip the puff peppers into. "Go get it."

Josh stared at Drake. Why did *he* have to get the bag? Why not Drake? "No!" he said. "What if it's rigged to explode?"

"Get the bag!" Drake rolled his eyes and pushed his brother toward the bag.

Josh stopped himself just as he was about to slam into the peppers. What if it was a trap? He waved his hands over the top of the bag, careful not to touch it. Then he poked it with his finger, jumped back, covered his head, and shrieked. After the exploding corn dog, there had been ringing in his ears for days. The last thing he needed was another blast in the face.

Nothing happened.

What is Josh doing? Drake wondered. They had to hurry. "Just grab it!" Drake hissed.

Josh took hold of the bag and ran, screaming, into the hall. He almost knocked Drake over in his rush to escape from Megan's terrifying bedroom.

The brothers were sound asleep that night when Megan burst into their room at two o'clock in the morning, wearing a pink pajama top and pink camouflage pajama pants. She turned on the lights, wrinkling her nose. The room smelled like boy.

"Get up," Megan yelled. She held a full-loaded super soaker gun in front of her and blasted Drake in the face with ice-cold water. Then she did the same to Josh.

"Megan," Drake screamed, wiping water off his face.

"What's the matter with you?" Josh rubbed his eyes and patted his wet pajama top.

Megan pointed her super soaker at them and stood her ground in her fuzzy pink slippers. "I want my Peruvian puff peppers," she said.

Drake and Josh exchanged sly looks. Drake stifled a laugh.

"Peruvian puff peppers?" Josh said, innocently, leaning his chin on his fist.

Drake wore a gray T-shirt and blue plaid pajama pants. He pretended to be confused. "Is that a band? I'm afraid I'm not familiar with their work."

Josh got out of bed and tried to look tough in his flannel pajamas. "Yeah, and I'm afraid we're going to have to ask you to leave." He took Megan by the arm and tried to lead her out of the room.

Megan dropped her water gun and grabbed Josh's wrist. She spun him around and flipped him over in one smooth move. Josh was trapped, facedown, on his bed.

The next thing Josh knew, Megan was spanking him!

"Owwwww," Josh screamed. Megan spanked him once for each syllable as she yelled. "I want my Peruvian puff peppers now!"

"Owwwww!" Josh screamed some more, kicking his legs. But Megan kept spanking.

Drake jumped out of bed and came to Josh's rescue. He pulled Megan away from Josh and stood between them. "Knock it off!" he yelled.

Megan fumed. She glared at the two of them for a second before grabbing her super soaker. She blasted Drake and Josh in the face one more time before stomping out of the room, slamming the door behind her.

CHAPTER EIGHT

Finally, it was the day of the Salsa Fest. Latin music played. Strings of garlic, onions, and chili peppers hung from the booths, and there were salsa and chips everywhere. People wandered from booth to booth, sampling them all. Judges carried scorecards and made notes as they tasted. The Yatsabishi plasma screen TV was mounted on a platform, surrounded by a yellow cardboard sun and covered with a big red bow.

Megan stood behind her booth, wearing a glittery red-and-black top. A judge approached, tasted Megan's salsa, and made a note on her clipboard. "Mmmm," she said. "Very good salsa."

"Thank you." Megan smiled sweetly at the judge, then at Drake and Josh, who were in the booth right next door.

Drake wore his "Knock on Wood" T-shirt for good luck. Josh went for the more dignified look — a navy blue polo shirt. They stopped glaring at Megan when a second judge came up to their booth.

He dipped a chip in the salsa and tasted. His tie was covered with pictures of chili peppers. Clearly, this guy took his salsa seriously. "Ohhhh," he said, nodding. "This is excellent. Superb!"

Walter and Audrey looked over the judge's shoulder. They wanted all three of their children to do well in the contest.

Josh could tell that Megan had heard the compliment. He smiled modestly. "We try," he said.

"Yeah we do," Drake added. He wasn't so modest. Their salsa rocked! The Peruvian puff peppers had made their TV-winning salsa even better.

"Well, you succeeded," the judge said. He marked his scorecard.

Josh patted Drake on the back. That was the last of the judges to taste their salsa, and the last one to say how good — no, how *superb* — it was. Of course all of them had complimented Megan's salsa, too, but they were just being nice because she looked like a sweet little girl — if only they knew.

But this time, Drake and Josh had stolen her secret weapon. Not only were they going to win, but they also were finally going to beat Megan.

The brothers grinned at each other and then at the TV. In a few short hours, that beautiful piece of electronic equipment would have a new home — their bedroom!

The judges huddled in the middle of the room. The contestants stood around, nervously waiting for the scores to be calculated. Finally, the head judge nodded at Mr. Holland, the Salsa Fest host. He stood at the podium, next to the TV.

"All right, if I can please have your attention," Mr. Holland said. "I see that all the judges have finished scoring the salsas, and now the time has come to announce the winner of this year's competition."

There was light applause, then everyone went quiet. The head judge finished making notes on a clipboard, then walked over to Mr. Holland and handed him the final scorecard.

This was it — the big moment.

Megan ran and stood with her parents. She wanted to be right up front when the winner was announced.

"And the winner for best traditional salsa, who will also take home this beautiful forty-five-inch Yatsabishi plasma screen television, is . . ." Mr. Holland paused for an agonizing minute.

Josh held his breath. Drake drummed his fingers on the table.

". . . the team of Drake Parker and Josh Nichols! Come on up here, boys!"

They won! The Parker-Nichols brothers were a winning team! The brothers ran to the podium and shook hands with Mr. Holland. He handed Josh the winner's plaque.

"Congratulations," Mr. Holland said.

"Thank you!" Drake and Josh said at the same time.

"Thank you very much," Josh said with a big smile. How cool was this? Not only had he and his brother won the contest, but they also had finally beaten Megan at something.

The crowd applauded. Walter and Audrey beamed. Megan had a sly smile on her face.

As the clapping died down, Megan yelled, "Hey! What's your secret?"

Others chimed in. "Yeah, tell us your secret."

"I'm sure we'd all love to know," Mr. Holland said, clapping.

Drake and Josh exchanged looks. Should they tell?

"Go ahead," Drake said to Josh. He was mentally rearranging their room to make sure the TV could be seen from his loft bed *and* the couch. "We already won."

Drake was right. They had won. And Megan had lost. Just to be nice, though, Josh would let her in their room once in a while to watch a movie. But first, he had to share his secret.

"All right." Josh proudly stepped up to the microphone. "Well, there are many secrets to making our fine salsa, but the most important is the utilization of the rare Peruvian puff pepper."

Mr. Holland's face fell. There were gasps in the audience, and the judges started whispering to one another. Megan smiled knowingly.

"The Peruvian puff pepper?" Mr. Holland asked, with a concerned expression.

Josh was suddenly worried. "Yeah," he answered.

"Why, is there a problem?" Drake asked.

The judges rushed over and formed a huddle with Mr. Holland. "I know. I know," he said, before turning back to the microphone. "Look, I'm very sorry," he said, "but the Peruvian puff pepper has been illegal in the United States since it was proven to cause kidney failure and/or chapped lips." Mr. Holland patted Josh on the back. "Boys, I'm afraid we're going to have to disqualify your salsa."

People in the audience rubbed their lips, checking for chapping.

Megan pretended to be sad for her brothers. "Awwww," she groaned.

The boys stood stunned and speechless while Mr. Holland checked his clipboard again.

"Which means that our grand prize goes to our second-place finalist," he said. "Miss Megan Parker!"

There was big applause from the crowd as Megan ran up to the podium. She tugged the plaque from Josh's hands, hitting him in the chin with it as she raised it over her head. Josh and Drake gaped at her, openmouthed. They hadn't beaten her. She had beaten them.

Megan had pranked her brothers — again!

"Thank you," Megan said over the applause. She held the award high over her head so everyone could see it. "How great is this day?"

As soon as the applause died down, Drake and Josh pulled Megan aside so no one else would hear.

"Okay, Megan . . ." Josh said, furiously.

"You set us up, didn't you?" Drake asked.

"What," Megan said, giving her brothers a "get a clue" look. "You think I purposely got the Peruvian puff peppers, knowing you'd steal them from me and use them in your own salsa, just so I could point it out to the judges, get you disqualified, and then walk away with the Yatsabishi plasma screen TV for myself?" Megan asked.

The guys stared at her blankly. It wasn't until that moment that they realized just how elaborate Megan's evil plot had been. And they had fallen for it every step of the way.

Megan grinned at her brothers. Maybe if they were really nice to her, she'd let them into her room once in a while to watch a movie — but then again, maybe not. "C'mon," she said, "I'm not *that* smart."

But she was, Drake realized.

Oh yeah, she was, Josh thought.

One little girl against two guys. And they had lost. Again.

CHAPTER NINE

That night Megan hung out in her room knitting and enjoying her new forty-five-inch Yatsabishi plasma screen television, mounted on the wall.

Audrey and Walter came in to check on her. "Hi, baby," Audrey said.

"Hey, Megan," Walter added.

"Oh, hi!" She smiled sweetly.

"How do you like your new plasma screen?" Audrey asked.

"Love it," Megan said.

"What are you watching?" Walter asked.

"Oh, just a show that teaches kids how we can all work together to help our environment," Megan said.

Audrey and Walter exchanged proud smiles. Megan was such a sweet little girl, they thought. She was always thinking about how to make the world a better place. If only her brothers would follow her example.

"How sweet," Audrey said.

"Well, we don't want to interrupt." Walter turned toward the door.

"Hey, where are Drake and Josh?" Megan asked, innocently.

"They're repainting the walls because of all that salsa they splattered everywhere," Audrey said.

"Well, it's nice that they're finally taking responsibility for their actions," Megan said.

"True. 'Night, baby." Audrey kissed Megan on the forehead.

"Yeah, good night," Walter said.

As soon as the door closed behind her parents, Megan picked up a remote control hidden under her knitting and pressed a button. The plasma screen was suddenly tuned into the kitchen, where Drake and Josh painted — and argued.

Megan picked up a bowl of popcorn and sat back against her pillows, crossing her fuzzy pink-slippered feet.

". . . like you're doing any better," Drake said.

"I never do anything, and you always get me into trouble." Josh wiped the sweat off his forehead.

"You know we wouldn't be in this mess if you hadn't been making your salsa," Drake said.

"Oh, making *my* salsa." Josh dipped his roller in the paint.

Megan giggled when Drake grabbed his roller and ran it over Josh's face. Josh lunged toward Drake and sloshed paint on his arm. Soon they were wrestling on the kitchen floor, covered in paint, and making an even bigger mess.

Megan leaned back and sighed happily. "My favorite show," she said.

Part Two:
The Bet

Prologue

Josh Nichols hung out in the kitchen, doing his homework and having an after-school snack. "I've got to say, I'm really glad Drake's my stepbrother."

Drake Parker kicked back on the recliner chair in his bedroom, a history book on his lap. "I'm really glad someone invented pizza," he said, taking a big bite of a slice. "Oh, and bikinis." He grinned, nodding. "Yeah, bikinis are cool."

Josh looked up from his homework. "But when you have a brother around the same age as you, sometimes it gets a little competitive."

Drake sat up and closed his book. "Last week, Josh challenged me to see who can hold his breath the longest," he said.

"We had this contest to see who could hold their breath longer." Josh remembered. "After two minutes . . ."

Drake took another bite of his cheese-and-pepperoni slice. "I won," he said.

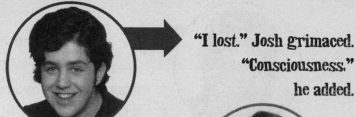

"I lost." Josh grimaced. "Consciousness," he added.

Drake laughed. Josh was too easy to fool. "I was breathing through my nose the whole time," he said.

"Oh and then there was the milk challenge," Josh said, remembering yet another brother vs. brother contest.

"I bet Josh my allowance that he couldn't chug an entire gallon of milk." Drake shook his head in disbelief. "But he did it. I lost."

Josh played with his pencils, pretending they were having a sword fight. Then he looked at his glass of milk and made a face. "I threw up," he said.

"He puked!" Drake said, laughing.

Josh shrugged, remembering his win. "It was worth it," he said with a smile.

Drake shrugged. He might have lost the bet, but Josh puked. "It was worth it," he said with a smile.

CHAPTER ONE

Drake wandered into the kitchen in search of breakfast. He could see Josh through the pass-through window into the living room. He was playing video games, as usual.

Drake poured himself a bowl full of multicolored, sugary Frosted Fruity-O's — his favorite cereal. Reaching past the soda for the milk in the refrigerator, Drake got an excellent idea. Instead of milk, he poured soda over his Frosted Fruity-O's.

Josh was focused on his video game — working the controls with the fastest thumbs in San Diego. He had a huge smile on his face as he blasted through an obstacle and moved up to the next level.

Drake tasted his new breakfast concoction. "Hmm," he said. It wasn't quite right. He found the sugar bowl and added a spoonful. Then he shrugged and added a few more. You could never have too much sugar, could you?

Drake's quiet breakfast was interrupted by Josh's screams from the living room.

"Yes, yes, yes!" Josh yelled. He was totally focused on his game, punching buttons on his game control. "You ain't no competition for Joshie!" he said to the TV. "Look out now!"

He dropped the game controls, raised his hands in the air, and turned from side to side. "And there it is!" Josh yelled. "Switching to the handheld!" He grabbed his handheld game, punching the buttons frantically. "Yeah, look out red turtle shell," he said to the game. "Yeah! Missed me, sucker!"

Drake ignored him. He was used to Josh's goofball video-game play-by-plays. He tasted his cereal again, then picked up the sugar bowl and dumped all the sugar on top. He stirred before tasting it again. He was right. You couldn't have too much sugar. "Sweet," he said, pleased with his new creation. Then he grabbed a donut and took a bite, getting the white powder all over his face.

Their mother, Audrey, rushed into the living room, pulling on her raincoat. "I am so late," she said. "Hey, can one of you boys do me a favor?" She threw her purse over her shoulder.

Drake didn't look up from his cereal. Josh's eyes never left his video game.

Audrey put on an earring and looked through a file folder before shoving it into her bag. She hadn't heard a "no" from either one of the guys. And she didn't have time to wait for a "yes."

"Megan is down the street playing at Eddie's house," Audrey said. "And it's about to pour down rain."

Drake grunted.

Josh mumbled.

"So one of you guys needs to take this umbrella over there and walk her home, okay?" Audrey continued, grabbing her keys.

This time Drake mumbled and took another bite of his sugary cereal.

Josh grunted and jumped another turtle shell.

"Here's the umbrella," Audrey said, setting a big black umbrella down next to the couch. "Thanks, guys." She rushed out the front door.

Drake took another bite of the donut. "Josh, you

better take the umbrella and go get Megan," he said with his mouth full. Powder drifted down onto his vintage "Tijuana, Mexico" T-shirt.

"Okay." Josh didn't look up. He had switched back from his handheld game to the one on the TV screen without missing a beat. "See you when you get back with Megan," he yelled.

CHAPTER TWO

Rain poured outside. Lightning flashed, followed by a boom of thunder. Josh didn't notice — he was playing a video game, and he was about to trample his previous record. His thumbs danced over the controls.

Drake lounged lazily on the sofa, eating a bag of chips. He didn't understand why Josh loved video games so much, but it could be kind of fun to watch him play. Josh was totally into it.

"Oh, yeah. Oh, yeah. Joshie's going to get you!" Josh yelled to the TV.

"Jump the mushroom." Drake pointed with a potato chip.

But no one could tell Josh how to play this game. He was an expert. "I'll jump the mushroom when it's mushroom-jumping time," he said, not taking his eyes off the TV screen.

Drake shrugged. He was only trying to help. He picked up a bottle of chocolate syrup and squirted some directly into his mouth.

The front door opened. Megan stood in the door-way while thunder and lightning crashed behind her. She was totally soaked. Water dripped down her face and from the tips of her long, dark hair. The monkey on her flowered T-shirt was drenched, as were her shoes, her black jeans, and everything else she wore. She slammed the door behind her, trying to get her brothers' attention.

"Hello?" she yelled, stomping over to the couch and making squelching noises with her wet sneakers.

Her brothers didn't look up.

"Helloooo!" she yelled again, louder and angrier this time.

Drake turned and looked at her. "Oh, yeah," he said with his mouth full. "This is for you." He handed her the umbrella.

Megan glared at it, furious, while Drake squirted more chocolate syrup into his mouth, and Josh focused on his video game.

Just then Audrey got home from work. Lightning flashed behind her as she closed the front door, a wet umbrella in her hand. She took one look at Megan and realized what had happened. Megan had walked home from Eddie's house in the pouring rain because neither one of the guys was willing to get off the couch and bring her the umbrella.

Audrey slammed her files down on the table. "Drake!" she yelled. "Josh!" Her purse hit the table with an angry bang.

The guys grunted. Their attention was on other things — junk food and video games.

Megan moved aside when Audrey marched over and snatched Drake's bag of potato chips.

"Hey!" he yelled, sitting up.

Then Audrey grabbed the remote control and turned off the TV.

Josh gasped, horrified. He was at level six! "What's up with that?" he asked.

"One thing!" Audrey shouted. "I ask you guys to do *one* thing for me. Look at Megan."

Megan opened her arms wide so they could see just how wet and cold she was.

Josh noticed her for the first time since she squelched over. "She's wet," he said, with a blank expression. What did that have to do with him?

Audrey rolled her eyes in frustration.

"Everyone can see I'm wet!" Megan yelled.

"You were too busy to go get your sister," Audrey said to Josh, taking the game controls out of his hand and holding it in front of her. "But you weren't too busy to play video games all day. . . ."

Drake saw an opportunity to stay out of trouble. He could blame his brother. "Josh," he said, drawing out Josh's name as if he were scolding him.

Audrey held up Drake's bag of chips. He wasn't getting off that easy. "Or to sit around eating twenty pounds of junk food."

"Drake," Josh scolded now.

"I keep telling you they're bad people," Megan said to her mom.

Audrey kept her focus on the guys. "Well? Do you have anything to say for yourselves?"

Uh-oh. Drake and Josh exchanged looks. Neither of them could think of anything to smooth things over with their mom, but Drake took a shot. "Well." He cleared his throat and sat up straighter, revealing a couch cushion covered with potato chip crumbs. "You see, I view this whole incident as a *learning* experience."

Audrey groaned and cut him off. "Upstairs. Both of you," she fumed. "You're grounded tonight."

Drake stood. *Grounded?* "But it's Saturday night!" he said.

"I'm supposed to meet Brian Horrowitz at the Magic Palace!" Josh whined.

"Go apologize to your sister, and then both of you," Audrey pointed, "upstairs."

Drake and Josh sighed. They could tell by the tone of their mom's voice that there was no getting out of this one. They walked over to Megan with their heads down and their shoulders slumped. Grounded on a Saturday night over an umbrella. It didn't seem right.

Megan dripped water and rage onto the carpet.

"Sorry," Drake mumbled.

"I'm sorry," Josh said.

Megan wasn't about to stop being mad after such lame apologies. She shook her head like a wet dog, letting her long, dark hair splatter rain all over them.

CHAPTER THREE

Josh sat on the couch in the bedroom he shared with Drake, playing another video game.

"You realize this is your fault," Drake said, pointing at Josh with a bag of cheese balls. The bag matched his orange T-shirt.

Before Josh moved in, the bedroom had been Drake's private paradise. It was kind of unfinished, with exposed beams and unpainted wallboard, but Drake liked it that way. He built a loft bed under the window, bought an old couch and comfy chairs at a yard sale, and filled the walls with all kinds of cool posters, road signs, and old license plates. There was nothing better than kicking back on his couch, his feet up on the coffee table, and watching the tube and chowing down on a pizza, a bag of chips, and a sugary dessert.

Then Josh moved in. Drake wasn't exactly thrilled to have to share his space at first. But he had to admit that it was easier to find things with a neat guy like Josh around — plus, Josh had a better stereo.

Still, there were times — like now when Josh was cemented to the couch while he played his video games — that sharing a room with Josh could be kind of a pain. Especially when he was grounded on a Saturday night because Josh couldn't leave his precious video games for one minute to bring Megan an umbrella.

My fault, Josh thought. "No. I do not realize that," Josh said, not missing a second of his game. He couldn't believe Drake was trying to put all the blame on him. He was at level six! You can't leave a game in the middle of level six. And Drake was just scarfing down chips and chocolate. He should have brought Megan the umbrella.

"You couldn't have stopped playing your video game for ten minutes to take her the stupid umbrella?" Drake asked, popping a couple of cheese balls in his mouth.

"Hey, number one, that umbrella is not stupid," Josh answered, his eyes focusing on Drake for one second before he turned back to his game. "My uncle bought it for me at Sea World." Drake interrupted him before Josh could move on to point number two — that it was Drake's fault.

"Oh, just face it, Josh. You are addicted to video games," Drake said.

"I am not *addicted* to them," Josh said. Then he smiled a small smile. "I am *in love* with them," he added, trying to lighten things up. But he did love video games.

Drake shook his head and reached into his snack bag again. "Well, how sad," he said, plopping into a chair.

"Not as sad as being addicted to junk food," Josh said, turning away from his game. "Which you are." He pointed to Drake's bag of cheese balls. "Man, do you have any idea how bad that stuff is for you?"

Was Josh seriously trying to say that Drake's little junk-food cravings were worse than Josh's obsession with video games? No way. Drake dropped his bag and picked up the video game control. "Oooh, look at me," he mocked, imitating his brother. "I'm Josh. I play video games all day long. Girls? No, thank you, ma'am. I got me a video game!" He dropped the control on the coffee table.

Two could play this game. Josh grabbed the bag of cheese balls and started stuffing his face. "Oooh, I'm Drake. Nutrition? Not for me!" He talked with his mouth full, spewing chunks of cheese balls across the room. "I'm just going to eat me a big old bag of cheese balls."

"Which you're allergic to," Drake said.

Uh-oh. Josh stopped chewing. His eyes got wide. He spit the half-chewed cheese balls into a tambourine that was on the coffee table. Then he grabbed a handheld vacuum cleaner and furiously ran it up and down his tongue, before blowing one last cheese chunk in Drake's direction. If he swallowed, his head could swell up like a melon.

Drake stared at Josh like he was crazy. So he liked junk food. Junk food was good. Josh was *obsessed* with video games. "Besides," Drake said, "food is a necessity. Video games have no value." He leaned back in his chair. Let Josh argue with that.

But Josh wasn't buying it. "Video games teach hand-eye coordination, which is why I now have catlike reflexes," Josh said, doing a little karate move with his hands.

Cat-like reflexes? Drake picked up a baseball and tossed it toward Josh. It bounced off his forehead a whole second before Josh tried to catch it.

"Yeah," Drake said. "*Dead* cat-like reflexes."

"I wasn't ready," Josh answered. He jumped to his feet and stood in front of his brother. Drake wasn't going to win this argument. The fact that Josh liked to play video games was nothing like Drake's junk-food mania. "Besides, I could quit video games a lot easier than you could quit junk food."

"Oh, reeeally?" Drake stood up and sniffed the air. It was time to put this argument to the test. "You smell that, Josh?" He sniffed again. "Smells like a bet to me."

Josh accepted the challenge. There was no way Drake could give up junk food. "No," he said, taking a big sniff. "I smell you losing a bet."

Yeah right, Drake thought. Josh would give up long before Drake even started to miss junk food. "Okay, hot pants, it's on," Drake said. "You give up video games. I give up junk food. The first one to cave loses."

"Okay, what happens when *you* lose?" Josh asked.

"When *you* lose, you have to . . ." Drake thought about it for a few seconds, then broke into a big grin. Another excellent idea! "Dye your hair pink."

"All right." Josh stuck out his hand. "Loser has to dye his hair pink."

The guys shook on it.

"So, are we starting right now?" Drake asked.

"Yeah," Josh growled. "We're starting right now!"

They each glanced sadly at the things they were giving up. Drake still had half a bag of cheese balls left, and Josh was in the middle of a game.

"Or we could start in the morning," Josh said.

Drake nodded. It would be a shame to let those cheese balls go stale. What a waste of cheese. "Morning works."

Josh dived for his video game controller and started playing frantically. Who knew how long Drake would hold out? He had to get plenty of games in while he could.

Drake grabbed the cheese balls and started stuffing his face. There was no way Josh could stay away from video games for more than a few hours, but he had to get in his salt and sugar while he could — just in case.

CHAPTER FOUR

Drake paced around the kitchen the next morning, waiting for Megan. Josh hopped from foot to foot. It was time to get this bet started.

"You got the contracts?" Drake asked when Megan finally showed up with some papers in her hand.

"Yep. Spell-checked and everything," she said.

Josh took a contract and started to read. Drake read over Josh's shoulder.

". . . must not play video games," Josh mumbled.

". . . cannot eat junk food of any kind," Drake read.

They kept reading. "And whoever caves *must dye*," Josh said.

"Must die?" Drake asked. Wasn't that taking things a little too far — even for Megan? What happened to their friendly bet?

Megan rolled her eyes and turned the page.

". . . his hair pink," Josh read, nodding.

"Ohhhhh," the guys said at the same time.

Megan pulled out two pens. "Sign, please," she said.

The guys signed on the dotted line, but that wasn't enough for Megan. She had to make sure this contract couldn't be broken. "Sign here." She pointed to the first paragraph. "And here," she said, pointing at another spot.

Drake and Josh signed and initialed.

"Not there!" She pulled the contract away from Drake, then pointed again. "Here. Signature here." She turned the page again. "One more initial here." Finally, she was satisfied. "Perfect," she said, taking the contract and heading upstairs to hide it in a safe place.

Later that day, Josh sat at the kitchen table, doing a jigsaw puzzle, bored out of his mind. He tried a blue piece, then threw it up in the air. It didn't fit. He tried another. Then another. He was surrounded by blue pieces, and none of them were right. "Stupid sky. You don't want to fit? Fine." Then Josh started to lose it. He stood up, yelling at the puzzle pieces. He grabbed the phone off the wall and used it to pound a piece of blue sky into the puzzle. "There! Who fits now?" he said.

"Hey, Josh." Megan came in and headed for the refrigerator. "So, how's the bet going?" she asked.

"Horrible! I've got to find something to replace video games, or I'm going to explode!"

"You could try exercising," Megan suggested, opening a bottle of water.

Exercising? Playing video games *was* exercise . . . for his hands. "This is no time for jokes, Megan!" Josh said.

Megan rolled her eyes and left the kitchen.

Josh got up and started pacing and biting his nails. "Got to play video games," he said desperately, coming unglued. "Can't play video games." He stopped short when he saw the microwave. It was sort of square, like a TV. It had a screen. It had buttons. "Ohhhh, micro-wave." He rushed to the machine and pressed a button. The microwave beeped. It made noise — like a video game! He pressed another button, then another.

Josh got excited! "Josh likes the microwave," he shouted. He started playing the appliance like a video game, pressing buttons using both hands.

"Reheat! Reheat," Josh said to the microwave. "Defrost. Defrost." He suddenly noticed the blender, next to the microwave, and included it in his game. "Ice crush, reheat, liquefy, grind," he said. He jumped from machine to machine, spinning around to make sure he got every button and adding his own sound effects to each machine's noises.

"Yes!" he shouted, swiveling from one machine to the other. "Defrost. Defrost. Stir. Warm. Blend. Blend." He was totally out of control. "Yeah!" he shouted. Josh was having fun now. "Ice crush," he yelled. "Grate. Blend."

Josh pumped his fist in the air. Oh, here was a new button. "Popcorn," he yelled. Then, "Reheat! Custom defrost!" He spun in place, reaching for the blend button only to find Drake standing in front of him shaking his head. Drake had seen the whole thing.

Josh opened his mouth to defend himself, but there was really nothing he could say. He was caught in the act of playing kitchen appliances like they were a video game.

Drake cracked up. "Pathetic," he said, pretending to be strong. But Drake's junk food cravings were starting to get to him, too — that's what drew him to the kitchen in the first place. He knew he couldn't eat anything, but at least he could visit his sugary snacks. And here was evidence that it wouldn't be long before Josh caved.

Josh knew he had lost it. He started to walk past Drake, but couldn't bring himself to leave his new game behind. He grabbed the blender, clutched it to his chest like it was a precious jewel, and ran upstairs.

As soon as he saw that Josh was gone, Drake dug through the cabinets, looking for his delicious junk food. He just wanted to look at the treats that would be waiting for him after he won the bet. He dumped bags of chips and packages of cupcakes on top of Josh's puzzle and eyed them with longing. "Oh, sweet cupcakes," he said, petting the package and then resting his cheek on it. "You feel so nice."

He didn't notice that Josh had come back downstairs and was watching him through the pass-through window. A minute ago Josh was losing it, but seeing Drake drooling over his stupid junk food steeled Josh's resolve. Drake was about to crack, and Josh was going to win this bet!

"I can't eat you now," Drake said, gently touching the bags of chips. "But don't worry, we'll be together again soon," he said.

"Yeah," Josh said, crossing his arms over this chest, "*I'm* pathetic." He left the room, laughing. As soon as

Drake took one little bite of a chip or a cookie, Josh was back to being the video-game king.

Drake watched him leave and then petted his special treats again. "It's okay, little snacks," he said, resting his cheek on the table. "That mean man is gone."

CHAPTER FIVE

The bedroom was pitch-black. Josh snored, fighting video game dragons in his sleep, while Drake dreamed about cupcakes. The alarm clock rang. Seven o'clock. Time to get up for school.

Drake banged it with his fist. It kept beeping. He banged it again. Then, without opening his eyes, Drake picked up a steel dumbbell and crushed the clock. Sparks flew, but the annoying beeping stopped.

"Josh, get up," Drake said, rubbing his eyes and stumbling down the ladder of his loft bed.

Josh kept snoring.

"Josh." Drake made his way across the room to turn on the light, heaving a bottle of water at Josh on the way.

"Ooof!" Josh rolled over and sat up. "Would you watch where you throw things at me," he yelled. "A little more to the left, and we could have had a serious problem."

Yeah, yeah, yeah, Drake thought. Right now he had a serious problem — incredibly bad morning breath and no toothpaste. "Dude, can I borrow your tooth-paste?" he asked.

"Yeah, no problem," Josh said. He started to get up, but then he got a look at Drake's face and fell back screaming. "Ahhhh . . . ahhhh . . ."

"What? What?" Drake asked. Had Megan sewn Josh's pajamas to the sheets again or given him a giant pj wedgie while he slept?

But Josh jumped up and raced across the room. Still screaming, he pulled a mirror off the wall and thrust it in front of Drake's face.

Drake checked himself out in the mirror. "Yaaaaggggghhhh!" he screamed. His face! His incred-ibly good-looking face! It was covered in an ugly, blotchy, red rash.

Audrey, Walter, and Josh looked on while Dr. Glazer from across the street examined Drake's face in their living room. "Well, this is going to sound a little odd," he said. "But the recent change in Drake's diet probably caused the rash."

"Wait a minute," Josh said. "You're saying he got that rash from *not* eating junk food?"

"Is that really possible?" Audrey asked.

"Sure. You see, his body was so accustomed to all the fat, sugar, and sodium that when he suddenly stopped, it resulted in this hideous facial rash," Dr. Glazer said.

Drake looked at him. *Hideous? Where is this guy's bedside manner?*

"No offense," said the doctor.

"Well, we really appreciate you coming by, Jeff. It's nice to have a doctor live across the street," Walter said.

"Yeah. Nice for you." Dr. Glazer pulled out a pad and jotted something down before ripping off the page and handing it to Walter. "Here's your bill."

Walter did a double take. "Three hundred dollars?" he asked.

"Yep." Dr. Glazer smiled. "See you." He picked up his medical bag and headed for the front door.

"Dude, wait!" Drake yelled desperately — the doctor was leaving without giving him the cure. "What about my hideous facial rash?"

"Well, I normally advise my patients to stay away from junk food." Dr. Glazer pulled a prescription pad and a pen out of his pocket. "But in light of your face, I suggest you eat some," said the doctor. "Perhaps a Doodle Cake." He ripped the page out of his pad and handed it to Drake before pointing at Walter. "Three hundred dollars," he reminded him.

Josh watched it all with a big smile, his fingers itching to pick up the video game controller. *Soon*, he told himself. *Soon.*

Drake checked out his blotchy face in a handheld mirror. "I can't believe this!" he moaned. "I mean, it makes me almost unattractive. What am I going to do?"

"Well, you heard the doctor," Audrey said.

"Yeah, bring in the junk food!" Josh pumped his fist in the air and did a couple of karate kicks before launching into a spazzy song and dance. "Joshie won the be-et! Drake's going to have pink ha-ir!" he sang, shaking his butt. "La, la, la, la, la, la!" He ended his dance with a bizarre version of the twist.

Drake stared at him. Josh was way too happy about this. But Drake had two choices — walk around with a hideous rash or dye his hair pink.

Megan came in carrying a package. "Hey, spaz," she said to Josh. "A package just came for you."

Josh took the box and read the return address on the label. "It's a present from Grammy!" he said, opening the box. "This day just keeps getting better and better!" He gasped when he saw what was inside. "It's a Gamesphere!" He pulled a round, red ball, about the size of a bowling ball, out of the box.

Drake looked over his shoulder. "No way. The Gamesphere doesn't come out for another three months."

"Never underestimate Grammy!" Josh said. Hadn't Drake learned that by now? Grammy had kicked Drake's butt in basketball the last time she was in town, and she was the one who sent Josh that lucky shirt last year. Josh could do anything in that shirt — until Megan gave it away.

Walter looked confused. "What's a Gamesphere?" he asked.

"Only the most sophisticated gaming experience ever created by humans!" Josh announced, holding it up. "And it's spherical!" He held it out in front of him so they could all appreciate its roundness. *"Spherical!,"* he repeated. "Oh man, I have got to plug this in." He set it down on the coffee table and turned the controls toward him.

Drake sat next to him, holding his breath. Josh had forgotten all about their bet in his excitement over the Gamesphere. Drake was going to win! And he was seconds away from being able to eat junk food again, not to mention cure his rash. "Good," Drake said. "Because the second you do, you lose the bet."

Josh winced. Man, he had to play with this thing. But Drake had to eat junk food first, or he'd lose the bet. "Ohhhh! But . . . but," he sputtered. In desperation, Josh grabbed the hand mirror and thrust it in Drake's face.

"Aaarrggghh!" Drake screamed.

"You have to eat some junk food right now," Josh said urgently. *Drake has to cave,* he thought. Josh had to play that Gamesphere. "The doctor said so!"

Drake grimaced and pushed the mirror away. "No way, man. Ain't going to happen," he said. "Now go ahead and play your ultra-cool new Gamesphere," he tempted.

"No!" Josh said. No way was Drake winning this

bet. Josh was not going to go to school with pink hair. He would never live it down. It was hard to believe, but the guys in the Physics Club could be merciless in their teasing.

"It's spherical," Drake said in a singsongy voice. He picked up the Gamesphere and waved it under Josh's nose.

"I know," Josh said miserably. His hands started to reach for it, even though his brain was telling him "no." Then he mustered all his determination. "But I'm not playing it!"

Drake was just as determined — hideous rash or no hideous rash. Josh was not going to win this bet. "And I'm not eating junk food."

Josh narrowed his eyes and thrust the mirror in Drake's face again. Drake screamed in horror, then took Josh by the shoulders and turned him so that he had to look at his Gamesphere. Now it was Josh's turn to scream.

Megan stood between her parents, watching Drake and Josh try to get each other to give up. She had a huge smile on her face. "This is the greatest day of my life," she said.

CHAPTER SIX

Drake crept into biology lab just before the bell rang, holding a book in front of his face to hide his rash. So far, no one had noticed. He slid as far down into his seat as possible and kept the book open, blocking his face.

Josh was just behind him. "Why don't you put the book down, Drake," Josh taunted. He slid into the seat next to Drake and rested his hands on the top of the desk. Josh was in serious video game withdrawal. His hands felt like they might jump off the ends of his wrists and go in search of a game controller.

Drake slammed the book hard onto Josh's hand and then immediately held it in front of his face again.

"Owww," Josh whined. But he had stopped thinking about video games, just for a second.

"There, I put it down. Happy?" Drake asked.

Josh glared at him and rubbed his sore hand. "Evil!" he said.

Wearing a white lab coat, their teacher, Miss Richardson, walked to the front of the room. "All right, class, let's begin," she said in a monotone as she drew a giant circle on the board.

"Behold. The human eye. This fascinating organ is the only visible extension of the brain." She droned on and on.

Josh couldn't pay attention. He fidgeted in his seat and held his forehead in pain. "I miss video games," he said to himself. "So, so much."

He looked up at Miss Richardson. Suddenly she was transformed. She was dressed all in white like a video-game princess.

Josh looked away and rubbed his eyes. But when he turned back, Miss Richardson was still a video-game princess. She spoke in a high, princess-like voice. Music played in the background.

"Josh, the evil dragon has locked me away in his castle," Princess Richardson said. "Press B to save me, Josh," she pleaded. "Press Beeeeeeeeeeeee!"

Josh tapped furiously on his desk. "I'm pressing it!" he yelled. "I'm pressing it."

"Josh? Josh?" Miss Richardson said in her normal voice.

"Yes, princess?" Josh asked, still in his fantasy land. The class laughed, and Josh snapped out of his daze. Miss Richardson looked normal again. It had only been a daydream.

"Please pay attention, Josh," she said. "And now, class, here's an actual, real human eye." She held an eyeball up in front of her so the whole class would see it.

It was met with lots of "Ewwws" and "Nasty!" The class was totally grossed out.

"Enough," Miss Richardson said angrily. "There's nothing disgusting about the human body." It was only then that she saw that Drake was hiding behind his book. "Drake, put that book down."

Drake hesitated, but he didn't have a choice. He lowered the book slowly. Maybe the class wouldn't even notice.

Miss Richardson took one look at his red, splotchy face and jumped back. "Oh . . . my . . . GOSH!" she screamed. She covered her mouth, threw the eyeball up into the air, and ran out of the room.

The whole class stared at Drake. They thought the eyeball was gross, but this was completely disgusting.

Yeah, right, Drake thought, as he raised the book in front of his face again. *There's nothing disgusting about the human body. Check out my face.*

After school, Josh sat on the couch in the living room, holding Grammy's present in his lap. "Gamesphere . . . Gamesphere," he said over and over to himself while he rocked forward and back. Forward and back. "Gamesphere."

Drake sat on the window seat staring into a hand mirror. "My face . . ." he moaned over and over. "Oh, my face."

"Gamesphere, Gamesphere, Gamesphere," Josh said, more quickly now. He was getting ready to crack.

Audrey and Walter passed through the living room on their way to the kitchen.

"Can you believe them?" Audrey asked.

"I know," Walter said. "There's no way Josh can keep this up. Drake's going to win this, easy."

"Are you kidding?" Audrey couldn't believe he thought Josh would give up first. "Drake's rash is spreading. He'll cave first."

Walter got cocky. "You want to bet on that?"

"You are so on," Audrey said. "What do you want to bet?"

They stared at each other, thinking.

Moments later, Megan showed up with a contract in hand.

"Loser *dies?*" Walter asked.

Megan rolled her eyes and turned the page.

"His hair pink," Audrey read.

"Sign here . . . initial here," Megan said. "Not there! Here. Another signature here."

Alone now, Josh still rocked on the couch, cradling the Gamesphere in his arms. Suddenly he snapped. He jumped to his feet. "That's it! This bet isn't worth it," he announced. "I have to play you," he said to the ball.

He was about to plug it into the television when Megan walked in.

"Josh!" she yelled, shocked.

Josh screamed and jumped a mile.

"What are you doing?" Megan yelled.

"I can't take it anymore!" Josh said. "I have to play the Gamesphere." He held the ball up in front of her. "It's spherical!" he whined.

Megan grabbed Josh by the collar and pushed him back down onto the couch. Watching her brothers fall apart over this bet was just too much fun — it couldn't end this easily. In fact, it was time to amp up the action. And Megan knew just how to do it.

"Will you calm down?" she asked.

"I can't calm down. I just can't handle it anymore," Josh insisted.

Megan slapped him.

Josh stared, stunned. But it took his mind off video games for a second. "Do it again," he said.

Megan slapped him again, harder this time. Josh calmed down a little.

"Thank you," he said, catching his breath.

"Josh, you can win this bet," Megan said. "You can do it."

"I don't think I can," Josh whimpered, petting the Gamesphere. He felt totally helpless. He *needed* video games. He needed to jump mushrooms and battle dragons. He had to save the princess!

Megan knew all about how to make someone crack. Hadn't she done it to Josh a whole bunch of times? "

All you have to do is sabotage Drake," she said. "Make him crack before you do."

"Sabotage?" Josh's face lit up. "That's good," he nodded. "That's really good."

Moments later Megan found Drake in his bedroom. She had worked on Josh. Now it was Drake's turn. She watched him dab ointment onto his rash as she gave him some advice.

"You have to sabotage Josh," she said.

"Sabotage?" Drake asked. *What did his sneaky little sister have in mind,* he wondered.

"Make him crack first," Megan said. "It's the only way to win the bet."

Drake grinned. "I like it." He turned to Megan. His face was even more red and blotchy than before, only now it had a dozen little globs of white ointment on it. "Is this noticeable?" he asked.

Megan shook her head no. *Let him believe it isn't,* she thought. This bet was about to heat up — big time — which meant a whole lot of fun for her.

CHAPTER SEVEN

After school the next day, Drake opened the door to his bedroom. He could see Josh standing across the room, but not much else. "Why is it dark in here?" he asked.

He stopped short when he turned on the light. His jaw dropped. Their bedroom looked like a magical candy kingdom. Bowls of candy sat everywhere. Garlands of popcorn were draped across the window. Licorice and taffy hung from the ceiling, and a path of gumdrops led to an inflatable kiddie pool filled with brown water. *Brown water?* Drake thought. Then it dawned on him. *Chocolate milk.*

With a proud grin, Josh stood in the middle of it all, wearing a top hat and holding a giant candy cane. He had spent a whole week's salary on candy, but it was worth it for the chance to play video games again.

"Josh, what did you do?" Drake sputtered.

"What do you mean, Drake?" Josh asked, innocently.

Drake gazed around in wonder. A dreamy smile spread across his face. "It's all candy," he licked his lips, "and junk food."

"Oh yeah," Josh agreed. "I suppose it is."

Drake picked up a fluffy pink square that sat on his loft bed. "Pillow?" he asked.

"Cotton candy," Josh said.

"But Josh, how did you do all this —"

Josh cut him off. As soon as Drake took one bite of candy, Josh was planning to run downstairs for his Gamesphere. Megan was brilliant! "Shhh." Josh held his giant candy cane in front of Drake's mouth. Drake's tongue almost reached out for a lick, but he caught himself in time.

"Don't ask. Just enjoy," Josh prodded.

Drake's dreamy smile faded. He threw the cotton-candy pillow down. "Nice try, Josh," he said, "but it's not going to work."

Like Josh was going to give up that easily. "But doesn't it all look so *gooooooood?*" he asked with a big smile.

Drake swallowed. It did look good. It looked better than good. It looked better than anything he had ever eaten in his whole life. But he wasn't going to cave. He couldn't. He put Megan's plan into action. "Not as good as . . ." He whipped the red ball out from behind his back. "Gamesphere!"

Josh gasped. "You tease," he hissed.

Drake plugged the Gamesphere into the TV. Lights started to flash. Electronic music played.

Josh stood openmouthed while a voice said, "Welcome to Gamesphere." A burst of warm light radiated from the TV. Josh was mesmerized. It was like he was paralyzed by the light.

"Hi," Josh said, meekly.

"Prepare for the ultimate gaming experience," the Gamesphere said, still in its soft, tempting voice. Then a monster truck announcer took over. "Now let's play some games!" it roared.

"You're killing me here," Josh moaned. His hands were twitching. They wanted to pull the controls out of Drake's hands.

"Hurts, doesn't it?" Drake asked.

Josh screamed and then ran over to the kiddie pool. Two could play this game. He dipped a cup in and drank. "Mmm," he said. "Chocolate milk."

Drake pretended to be unfazed. "Big deal."

Josh smiled and took a big bite out of the cup. "Chocolate cup," he said.

Drake shuddered. This was hard. But he wasn't about to be outdone. He had another trick ready: Sabotage, Plan B. He pulled out a fancy, glowing game controller. It had cost him every cent he had, but this would push Josh over the edge.

Josh's eyes got wide, and he gasped again. "You got a wireless Battlepad?"

"Yep." Drake nodded and pushed buttons as he walked around the room. "Look at me," he said, striding around the pool of chocolate milk. "Walking and playing. I'm playing the Gamesphere."

Josh wanted to reach out and snatch the Battlepad from Drake's fingers. He dug deep for willpower and starting shoving candy into his mouth. "Mmm," he said. "Marshmallows!"

Drake watched Josh shove two marshmallows into his mouth, then turned back to the game. "Woo-hoo!" Drake said. "Level two!"

"Loving that licorice!" Josh answered, piling it in with the marshmallows.

"Hey! I just warped," Drake said. He pretended not to notice the delicious candy Josh was eating. He couldn't wait to take a big bite of that cotton candy pillow, but first he had to get Josh to crack. "Man, look at those graphics."

Josh was getting desperate. He had to push Drake over the edge so he could grab that Battlepad. *He had to.* "Everybody loves gummy bears!" he said with his mouth full. Gummy bears went flying.

Drake forced himself to turn away from the gummy bears. He turned back to the game, but then back to Josh again. Gummy bears spilled out of Josh's mouth as Josh gazed at the Battlepad, then at Drake. The brothers stared at each other for a second, looks of disgust on their faces.

"Give me that!" they yelled at the same time.

Drake dropped the Battlepad and dove for the gummy bears, then the marshmallows, filling his mouth. *At last, sugar!* At the same time, Josh fell on top of the Battlepad and started playing the Gamesphere. He had an ecstatic smile.

After a few seconds Drake and Josh looked at each other. Suddenly, Josh dropped the controller. Drake dropped the food and spit out the giant marshmallow he had in his mouth.

"A-ha! You caved!" they said at the same time.

"You caved first," Drake said.

"You caved first," Josh insisted.

Drake reached over and knocked off Josh's top hat, sending it flying into the pool of chocolate milk.

They charged each other, started to wrestle, and fell into the pool. Chocolate milk flew everywhere as they flailed around in the pool, tried to stand, and then fell again. Drake got halfway out, and then Josh pulled him back in. Their hair and clothes were covered with chocolate milk.

They continued to splash around, trying to get a hold of each other in the slippery mess. Drake grabbed on to Josh's shirt and pinned him to the bottom of the pool, but Josh threw him off again and squirted a mouthful of chocolate milk into Drake's face.

They were still sputtering and struggling in the pool when Walter and Audrey ran in, knocking giant candy canes and marshmallow toadstools out of their way.

"Boys! Boys!" Audrey yelled, rushing over.

Walter tried to separate the guys, getting a face full of chocolate milk himself. "Guys! Guys!" he yelled. "What is going on?"

Finally, Drake and Josh stopped fighting and stood in the middle of the kiddie pool — surrounded by puddles of chocolate milk. They both starting talking at once, trying to make the case that the other one caved first.

"Josh turned the room into candy, and I love candy, and even my pillow is candy, and he ate the candy in front of me *and then Josh caved*," Drake said, all in one breath.

But Walter and Audrey could hardly hear him because at the same time, Josh was making his case. "Drake took out the Gamesphere, and then he started playing the Gamesphere, and then the Gamesphere started talking to me, and it was all," Josh switched to his Gamesphere voice, "hello, Josh." He took a breath and finished in his own voice. *"And then Drake caved."*

"You caved first!" Drake yelled.

"Excuse me, you caved first!" Josh yelled back.

Walter and Audrey looked at each other and back at the guys.

They were still arguing about who caved first when Megan came in with the contracts. "Hey," she yelled, trying to get everyone's attention. "Hey, HEY!"

The guys stopped arguing and looked at her.

"It doesn't matter who caved first," Megan said.

"Huh?" Drake asked.

"What?" Josh said.

"The contract says . . ." Megan started to read. "Whoever caves must dye his hair pink." She looked up with a proud smile. It didn't matter who won the bet. Megan knew she was the real winner. "You both caved, so you both have to do it."

"But I didn't —" Josh sputtered.

"But we never —" Drake added.

"Mom! Dad!" The guys whined. Their parents wouldn't really let Megan get away with this, would they?

But then they did.

"You boys signed a contract," Audrey said. "You made a commitment."

"You have to honor a commitment," Walter agreed.

"Yeah, about that." Megan held up her parents' contract. "Mom, you bet on Josh. Dad, you bet on Drake. They both lost."

"Yeah, but —" Audrey said.

"We didn't mean —" Walter added.

Drake gloated. If he was going to have to dye his hair pink, so were his parents. "You signed a contract."

Josh crossed his arms over his chest. If he and Drake had to dye their hair pink, then so did Mom and Dad. "You have to honor a commitment," he added.

CHAPTER EIGHT

Megan was putting her books into her backpack the next morning when Walter came downstairs, followed by Audrey. Megan cracked up. Both of them had shocking pink hair.

Audrey stopped at the bottom of the stairs and yelled. "Drake! Josh! You'll be late for school."

Drake and Josh trudged downstairs — their hair was the same bright pink color as their parents'. They all looked at each other for a second. They were in full agreement on one thing — no more bets! At least not if Megan was writing the contracts.

"Okay, I was wrong," Megan said with a grin. "*This* is the best day of my life."

Audrey frowned at her. "Just get in the car," she said.

Megan skipped out the front door.

"See you, boys," Walter said.

"'Bye," Audrey added.

Drake and Josh were alone.

"So, when do you think this pink will wear off?" Josh asked.

"I don't know. A few weeks. Months," Drake answered.

Josh sighed. "School's going to be rough," he said, but at least he wouldn't have to face the kids alone. Drake had pink hair, too.

"Oh yeah," Drake agreed.

"Well, let's go," Josh said.

"Nah, I'm going to get some breakfast. I'll meet you at school," Drake said.

Josh hesitated. The last thing he wanted to do was walk into school with pink hair alone, but he hated to be late more than anything. "Okay," he said. "See you."

Drake watched Josh leave, then checked to make sure he was really gone before taking off his pink wig.

He checked himself out in the mirror. The horrible, red rash was gone now that he was eating junk food again, and his brown hair looked terrific. He felt a little bad about tricking Josh after all they had just been through, but no way was he going to walk around with pink hair over a silly bet.

He shook his head, thinking about Josh and his parents. They had actually dyed their hair. "Idiots," he said, and grabbed a donut before leaving for school.